Todd's Box

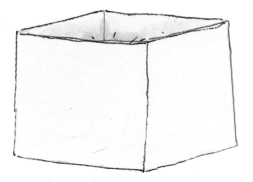

Todd's Box

Paula Sullivan

Illustrated by
Nadine Bernard Westcott

**Green Light Readers
Harcourt, Inc.**

Orlando   Austin   New York
San Diego   London

Look, Mom! I can dig in the sand.

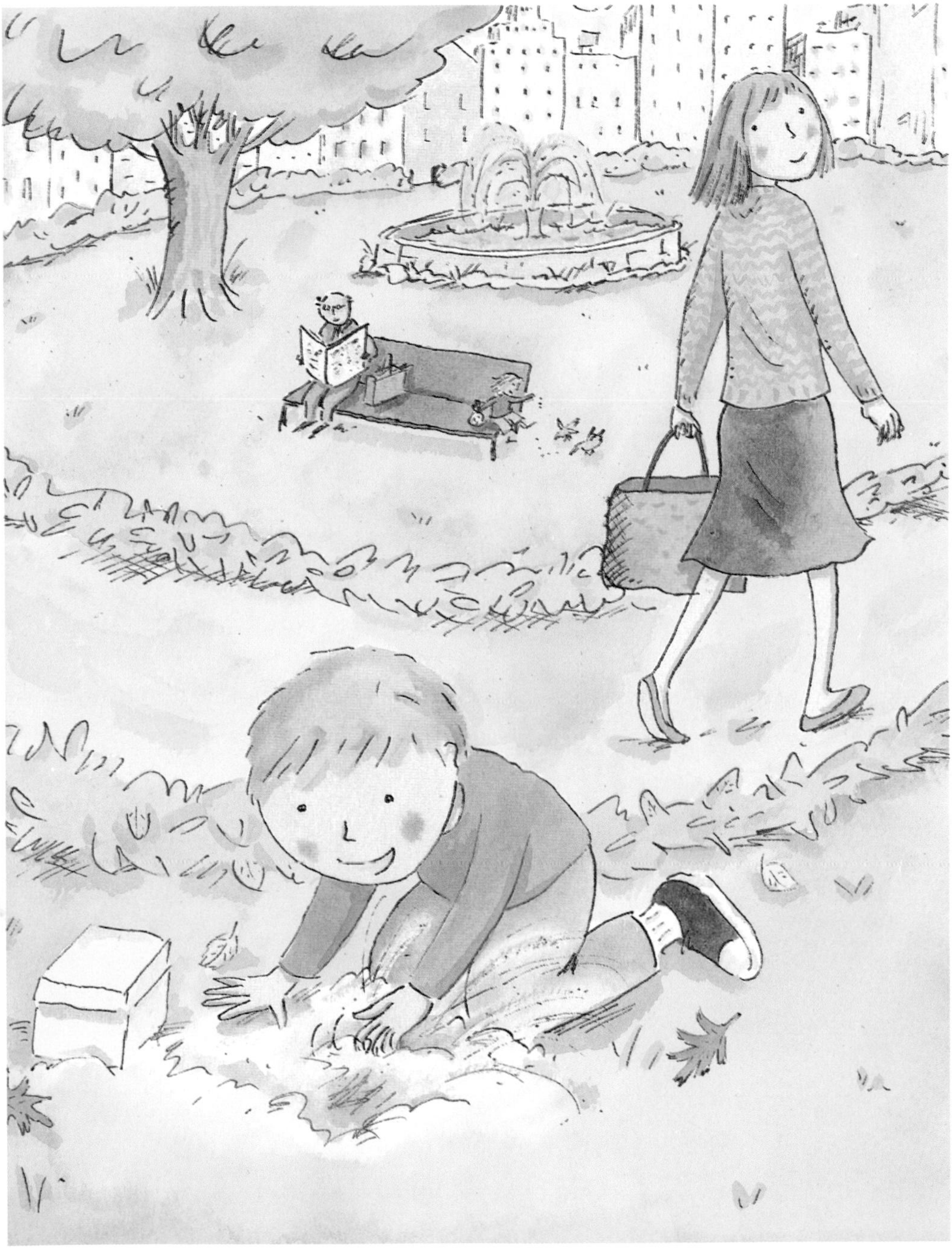

Not now, Todd.

Look, Mom!
I can climb the rocks.

Hop off, Todd.

Look, Mom!
I can catch this ant.

Don't pick it up, Todd.

Look, Mom!
I can run by the pond.

We have to go, Todd.

Look, Mom!
Here's a gift for you.

Look in and see.

Oh, Todd!
It's a box of surprises!

Think About It

1. Why does Todd say "Look, Mom!" so many times?

2. How does Todd surprise his mom?

3. Why is Todd's mom so surprised?

4. What do you think Todd's mom learns in this story?

5. Have you ever picked up things on a walk? What did you find?

ACTIVITY

Pack Your Suitcase

Pretend you are going on a walk like Todd.

What special things will you find along the way?

Make a suitcase to carry them all!

construction paper

pipe cleaners

magazines

scissors

crayons

hole punch

glue

1 Fold the paper in half.

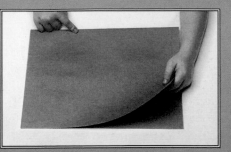

2 Make a handle for each side.

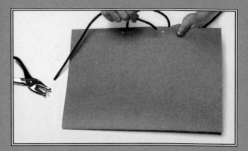

3 Fill your suitcase with pictures.

Ask a friend to guess what is in your suitcase. Then show and tell what you have inside!

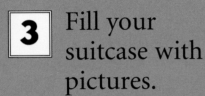

Take a Walk

Walk with a friend in the park or in the school yard.
Make a list of all the things you see and hear.

A Nice Gift

Todd gave his mother a gift. What gift would you
like to give someone in your family? Draw a picture
of your gift and write a sentence about it.

Meet the Illustrator

Nadine Bernard Westcott started drawing when she was very young. For *Todd's Box*, she first drew the pictures with a special black pen. Then she painted the pictures with bright pastel colors. She says she likes to draw pictures for children because it's fun!

Nadine Bernard Westcott

www.hmhbooks.com

First Green Light Readers edition 2004
Green Light Readers is a trademark of Harcourt, Inc., registered in the
United States of America and/or other jurisdictions.

Library of Congress Cataloging-in-Publication Data
Sullivan, Paula.
Todd's box/Paula Sullivan; illustrated by Nadine Bernard Westcott.
p. cm.
"Green Light Readers."
Summary: Todd surprises his mother with a box full of objects that
he has collected while walking with her to catch a bus.
[1. Walking—Fiction. 2. Mothers and sons—Fiction.]
I. Westcott, Nadine Bernard, ill. II. Title. III. Series: Green Light Reader.
PZ7.M788193To 2004
[E]—dc22   2003012865
ISBN 978-0-15-205093-1
ISBN 978-0-15-205094-8 pb

SCP   10 9 8
4500434473

Ages 4–6
Grade: 1
Guided Reading Level: E–F
Reading Recovery Level: 8

Green Light Readers
For the reader who's ready to GO!

"A must-have for any family with a beginning reader."—*Boston Sunday Herald*

"You can't go wrong with adding several copies of these terrific books to your beginning-to-read collection."—*School Library Journal*

"A winner for the beginner."—*Booklist*

Five Tips to Help Your Child Become a Great Reader

1. Get involved. Reading aloud to and with your child is just as important as encouraging your child to read independently.

2. Be curious. Ask questions about what your child is reading.

3. Make reading fun. Allow your child to pick books on subjects that interest her or him.

4. Words are everywhere—not just in books. Practice reading signs, packages, and cereal boxes with your child.

5. Set a good example. Make sure your child sees YOU reading.

Why Green Light Readers Is the Best Series for Your New Reader

• Created exclusively for beginning readers by some of the biggest and brightest names in children's books

• Reinforces the reading skills your child is learning in school

• Encourages children to read—and finish—books by themselves

• Offers extra enrichment through fun, age-appropriate activities unique to each story

• Incorporates characteristics of the Reading Recovery program used by educators

• Developed with Harcourt School Publishers and credentialed educational consultants